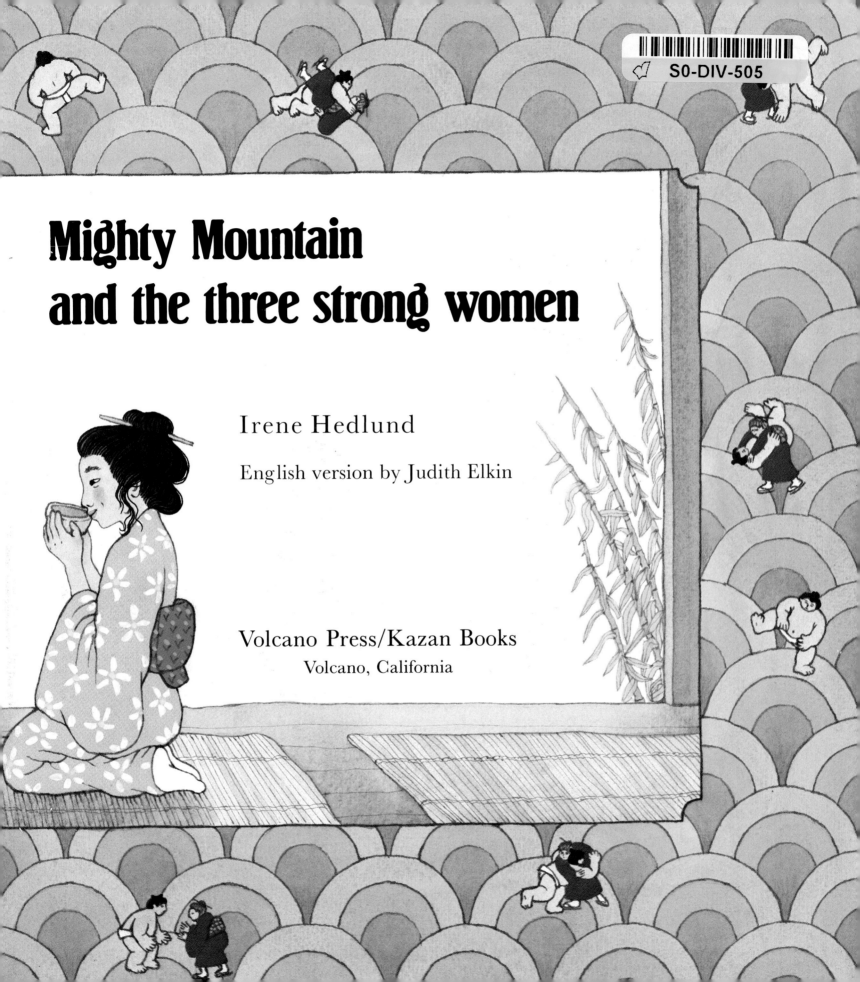

Mighty Mountain
and the three strong women

Irene Hedlund

English version by Judith Elkin

Volcano Press/Kazan Books
Volcano, California

Many years ago in a small village in Japan,
a huge baby was born. He was so big
that everyone called him Baby Mountain.

By the time he was twelve, he was the biggest,
strongest boy in the school and the wrestling
champion of the whole village. The people in the
village were proud of their enormous champion
and called him Mighty Mountain.

One warm autumn day, Mighty Mountain
decided he must leave the village. He would go to
the capital and become a famous wrestler. Every
year, the Emperor held a grand wrestling match
to find the strongest man in all Japan. Mighty
Mountain was sure that he could win.

It was a long walk to the capital and Mighty Mountain strode along, humming to himself. At each step, the ground shook, birds fell from the trees and animals scurried away in terror.

Mighty Mountain didn't even notice. He was too busy thinking how wonderful he was. Everyone loved him because he was so big and strong. He was quite sure that he was the best-looking wrestler in all Japan, but of course he was far too modest to boast about it.

Just then, Mighty Mountain noticed a girl filling her bucket with water. She was very pretty, with pink cheeks, shining black hair and sparkling eyes.

As the girl climbed on to the footpath in front of him, Mighty Mountain grinned to himself. What fun it would be to tickle her and make her spill the water. Perhaps he could walk home with her and help her to carry the bucket.

Mighty Mountain crept up behind the girl and poked a giant finger in her side. The girl squealed and giggled, but she didn't spill the water. Then, before Mighty Mountain could move away, she trapped his massive hand under her arm.

Mighty Mountain was delighted. 'Playful as well as pretty,' he thought. He tried to pull his hand away, but it wouldn't budge. He pulled harder.

'Let me go,' he laughed. 'You're very strong for a girl, but I don't want to hurt you.'

'Oh, don't worry about that,' giggled the girl, 'I love strong men. Try pulling harder.' She smiled sweetly at him.

But the harder he pulled and tugged, the tighter the girl's grip seemed to get. She began to walk on, dragging the wrestler behind her.

'Please, let me go,' he begged. 'I'm Mighty Mountain, strongest and bravest of all the wrestlers and I'm on my way to take part in the Emperor's Wrestling Match.'

'Oh, you must come and meet Grandma, then. You seem tired. Let me carry you to our house.'

'Certainly not. Just let me go!'

The girl stopped and seemed to look right inside him.

'I'm sure you're a good wrestler,' she said kindly, 'but what will you do when you meet someone who is really strong? You've got three months before the wrestling match. I know because Grandma thought of taking part. If you come home with me now, we could make you into the strongest man in all Japan. Otherwise, you will only spend all your time in bad company and lose what little strength you've got.'

'I don't need help from you, or Grandma, or anyone else,' roared Mighty Mountain, but a tiny shadow of doubt had begun to creep into his mind. He *was* feeling tired and his knees had gone quite weak. If he refused to go with the girl, she might easily break his arm or throw him down the steep mountainside.

He nodded wearily. The girl let him go. He peered down miserably at his red, swollen hand and wondered what he had let himself in for.

They came at last to a small thatched hut high up in the mountains. The girl pointed to two tiny feet in the doorway. Grandma was having her afternoon nap.

Round the corner of the hut came a woman carrying a cow on one shoulder. It was the girl's mother, back from working in the fields. When she caught sight of them, she put the cow down and hurriedly brushed the cowhair off her clothes.

'The poor cow gets sore feet, if I let her walk on the stony paths,' she explained to the astonished Mighty Mountain. 'Who is this nice young man, Kuniko?'

Kuniko told her. The two women walked around the wrestler, looking him up and down. Mighty Mountain giggled nervously and puffed out his chest and arms to show his huge muscles.

'Mm,' said Mother, 'he looks delicate. He needs some proper food.'

Then Kuniko called Grandma. She shouted very loudly because Grandma was a little deaf. The tiny feet started to kick furiously.

'All right, all right, I'm coming!'

A tiny, very wrinkled, toothless old lady shuffled out, leaning heavily on a stick. She stumbled over the roots of the great oak tree in the yard.

'Ow . . . ow . . . ow . . .' she muttered. 'My eyes aren't what they used to be. That's the third time this week I've bumped into that silly old tree.'

She put her thin arms round the trunk and pulled it straight out of the ground.

'Throw it away, dear,' she said to her daughter, 'I don't think my poor old back could manage it. Mind it doesn't get in anyone's way. You know how clumsy you are.'

Kuniko's mother threw the tree. It flew through the air like a rocket, getting smaller and smaller until it landed on the far mountainside.

Mighty Mountain could stand no more. His face went pale, his eyes glazed over and his massive legs trembled. Suddenly, with a terrific thump, he crumpled to the ground.

Mighty Mountain had fainted.

Grandma noticed him for the first time, as he crashed at her feet.

'Who's this?' she cackled.

Kuniko gently cradled Mighty Mountain in her arms.

'Poor weak man,' she whispered. 'Do you think we could get him ready for the ring in only three months?'

Grandma sighed, 'Well, it's not long,' she said 'and he's a feeble-looking fellow.' She bent down and flung him over her shoulder. Leaning heavily on her stick, she hobbled back into the hut and threw him on the bed.

The next day, the three women set to work.

Very early every morning, Kuniko dragged Mighty Mountain out of bed and made him bathe in the icy stream. Each day, Mother boiled his rice in less and less water, until he could eat food no ordinary man could even chew. Grandma made him work harder and harder and carry heavier and heavier loads.

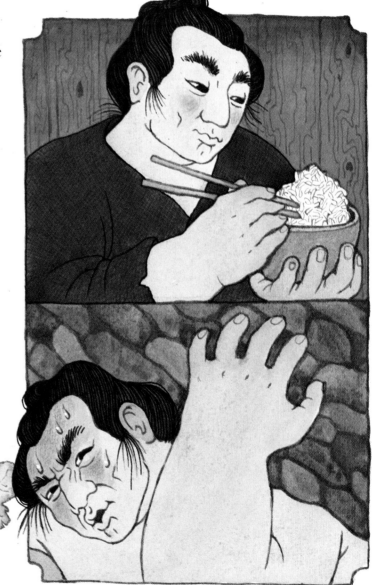

Every evening, Mighty Mountain practised wrestling with Grandma. Grandma was so old and frail that she couldn't do him too much harm. The exercise might even help her rheumatism.

As the days grew colder and colder and autumn turned to winter, Mighty Mountain got stronger and stronger, almost without noticing. Soon he could pull up trees almost as easily as Grandma could. He could even throw them, but not very far.

Before wrestling practice, Mighty Mountain stamped his foot on the ground. Then the villagers down below looked up at the winter sky and wondered why the thunder was rumbling round the mountains so late in the year.

One evening, Mighty Mountain managed to hold Grandma down on the ground for half a minute.

Grandma's face broke into a thousand wrinkles as she cackled loudly. Kuniko shrieked with excitement and hugged him, almost breaking his ribs. Mother slapped him on the back, making his eyes water.

They all agreed that Mighty Mountain was ready to take part in the Emperor's Wrestling Match.

'We want you to take the cow,' said Mother. 'Sell her and buy yourself a belt of silk, the thickest and heaviest you can find. If you wear it when you greet the Emperor, it will remind you of us and bring you luck.'

Mighty Mountain looked worried. 'I can't take the cow. How will you plough the fields?'

Grandma almost fell over laughing. Kuniko giggled, 'We don't use the cow for work. Mother is five times stronger than any cow. We only keep the cow because she's got such beautiful brown eyes.'

'She's very pretty,' agreed Mother, 'but it's hard work carrying her down to the valley every day to find grass.'

'Then if I earn any money at the Wrestling Match, you shall have it.'

Kuniko blushed, 'Oh, no,' she said, 'we can't take money from a stranger.'

Mighty Mountain grinned at her, bowed low to Grandma and asked if he could marry Kuniko and become one of the family.

Kuniko clapped her hands with joy. Grandma and Mother pretended to give the matter deep and serious consideration, then, with big smiles, they agreed. 'We'll even let you beat us at wrestling sometimes.'

The very next morning, Mighty Mountain tied
his hair in a fancy topknot, thanked Mother,
threw Grandma up in the air just for fun, and
playfully tickled Kuniko.

He ran off down the mountain carrying the cow
and waving until he could no longer see the
three women.

At the first town he came to, Mighty Mountain
sold the cow. She had never worked, so she was
good and fat, and fetched a high price. With the
money, he bought the thickest and heaviest silk
belt he could find. Then he headed towards
the capital.

Mighty Mountain hardly noticed the cold as he
crunched through the snow in his bare feet. He
was too busy thinking of Kuniko and Mother
and Grandma.

When he reached the Emperor's Palace, he found that the other wrestlers were already there. They were lazing about, preening themselves, eating large bowls of soft rice, telling fantastic stories and comparing their enormous weights and their huge stomachs.

No one took any notice of Mighty Mountain.

In the Palace Yard, the ladies-in-waiting and courtiers waited for the wrestling to begin. They wore layers and layers of clothes, so heavy with gold and embroidery that they could hardly move. The ladies-in-waiting wore thick white make-up, and the false eyebrows painted high on their foreheads made them look surprised all the time.

The Emperor sat as still as a statue and all alone behind a screen. He was far too aloof and dignified to be seen by ordinary people. The wrestling bored him. He much preferred reading and writing poetry and hoped the wrestling would soon be over.

The first match was between Mighty Mountain and Balloon Belly, a wrestler who was famous for his gigantic stomach.

With great ceremony, the two wrestlers threw a little salt into the ring to drive away evil spirits. Then they stood, legs apart, facing each other.

Balloon Belly rippled his enormous stomach then raised his foot and stamped the ground with a terrific crash. He glared at Mighty Mountain, as if to say, 'Beat that, weakling!'

Mighty Mountain glared back at Balloon Belly, thought of Grandma and stamped his foot. It sounded like a clap of thunder. The ground shook and Balloon Belly floated out of the ring like a giant green soap bubble. He landed with a thud in front of the Emperor's screen.

'The Earth God is angry,' Balloon Belly stammered, bowing low to the screen, 'I think there's something wrong with the salt. I had better not wrestle again this year.'

Five other wrestlers thought the Earth God might be angry with them, too, and decided not to wrestle.

When the next competitor was ready, Mighty Mountain was careful not to stamp his foot too hard. He just picked his opponent up round the waist and carried him out of the ring.

With a polite bow, Mighty Mountain placed the wrestler in front of the Emperor's screen. Then, one by one, he did exactly the same with all the other wrestlers.

The ladies-in-waiting looked more surprised than ever as they giggled delightedly behind their fans.

The Emperor's shoulders heaved with silent laughter and the plume on his head-dress wobbled in a most undignified manner. He hadn't seen anything so funny for years.

He put one royal finger through the screen and waggled it at the wrestlers who were sitting on the ground blubbering. He gave orders for Mighty Mountain to receive all the prize money.

The Emperor congratulated Mighty Mountain. 'But,' he whispered, 'I don't think you had better take part again next year. We don't want to upset these poor babies any more.' He looked at the heap of wrestlers and started giggling again.

Mighty Mountain agreed quite happily. He had decided that he would much rather be a farmer anyway, and he hurried off back to Kuniko.

Kuniko saw him coming from a long way off and ran to meet him. She hugged him carefully, then picked him up and carried him and the heavy bag of money halfway up the mountain. Then she put him down and let him carry her the rest of the way home.

The name of Mighty Mountain was soon forgotten in the capital. But the Emperor never really enjoyed another wrestling match and was always glad when it was over and he could get back to his poetry.

Now and again, the people in the village down below feel the earth shake and hear thunder rumbling round the mountains. But it's only Mighty Mountain and Grandma practising their wrestling.